Wibble Wobble
BOOM!

For Omar Williams
and Trudi Counce McClain
—M. A. R.

For Jasper. May you jump,
leap, and twirl your way through life.
—H. S.

Published by
PEACHTREE PUBLISHING COMPANY INC.
1700 Chattahoochee Avenue
Atlanta, Georgia 30318-2112
PeachtreeBooks.com

Text © 2022 by Mary Ann Rodman
Illustrations © 2022 by Holly Sterling

Design and composition by Adela Pons
Edited by Jonah Heller

The illustrations were rendered in pencil, colored pencil, monoprinting,
acrylic paint, and digital.

Printed and bound in July 2022 at C&C Offset, Shenzhen, China.
10 9 8 7 6 5 4 3 2 1
First Edition
ISBN: 978-1-68263-220-8

Cataloging-in-Publication Data is available from the Library of Congress.

Wibble Wobble BOOM!

PEACHTREE
ATLANTA

written by
Mary ann
Rodman

illustrated by
Holly
Sterling

Jump. Leap. Twirl.
Jump. Leap. Twirl.

I swoop and swirl up the walk
to the Ice Center.
"Wait for me, Claire," calls Mom.

Today's my first ice-skating class. I'll
fly through the air, land on one foot,
and spin so fast you can't see me.
One little lesson and I'll be on TV!

"What's your name, sweetie?" says a lady
with a clipboard.

"Claire."

"You're a Snowplow," she says.

"I'm not a Snowplow. I'm a skater," I tell her.

"Snowplows are beginner skaters." The lady
smacks a name sticker on my chest. "Go get
your skates."

A man at the counter gives Mom brown skates.

"Those skates are ugly. I want white ones!" I say.

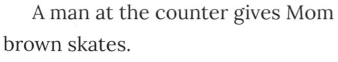

"Brown skates come with the lessons," says Mom. "If you like skating we can buy white ones."

"I like skating right now!" I tell her. But Mom doesn't listen.

A girl in a pink vest plops down next to me. Her sticker says "Olivia." *Her* skates are white.

She looks like a skater. I look like a Snowplow.

Two boys in hockey shirts clomp over.

"Why are your skates brown?" one of them asks.

"Why are yours black?" I answer.

"They're hockey skates!" the boys yell.

Whoosh-crunch.

A skater swoops across the ice to our bench.

"Hi, Snowplows. I'm your coach, Miss Nicole. Ready to skate?"

"Yeah!" we shout.

But we don't skate.

We stand up in skates, then sit down again.

Up, down.

Up, down.

This isn't skating. I want to skate!

"Good job," Miss Nicole cheers.
"Let's get on the ice."

I'll show Miss Nicole. I'm a real
a skater, not a Snowplow. I'll show
everybody!

I step onto the rink.

Wibble.

Another step.

Wobble.

What's wrong with my ankles?

Wibble. Wobble . . .

BOOM!

Woosh-crunch.

"Did everyone see Claire fall?" Miss Nicole calls.

"Yeah!" holler the Snowplows.

"She fell on her bottom, the right way to fall. Good job, Claire."

"But I fell," I say.

"All skaters fall," says Miss Nicole.
"Okay Snowplows, Claire and I will show
you how to get up."

I *scribble scrabble* up.

Falling is easy, but I want to skate!
Miss Nicole claps her mittens. "Line up everyone,
side by side."

Wibble. Wobble.
BOOM.

Wibble. Wobble.
BOOM.

Lining up takes a long time.

"Put your hands on your waist and march in place," says Miss Nicole. "Good job! Let's march in line to the other side." The other side is far, far away.

This isn't skating!

Wibble. Wobble.
    Wibble. Wobble—

Bump BOOM.

"You pushed me," yells Olivia.
"Did not."

Whoosh-crunch.

"Problem, girls?" asks Miss Nicole.
"No," we mumble. "Sorry."
"Let's stay farther apart," says Miss Nicole.
We *scribble scrabble* up and march away.

I *wibble wobble* to the side. Everyone is so far ahead. I hurry to catch up.

Wibble-wobble-wibble-wobble-

BOOM!

"Know why you're called a Snowplow?"
shouts a hockey boy. "'Cause you clean the
ice with your bottom!"

Skating is hard, not fun!
I *huff* and *puff* to the other side.

"Good job." Miss Nicole smiles.
"Now back where you started. One at a time."

My feet hurt, and I'm cold. I hide at the end of the line.
Maybe Miss Nicole will forget I'm here.

One by one, skaters *wibble wobble* away. When they go BOOM, Miss Nicole *whoosh-crunches* over to help.

I watch her feet.
Push, glide, slide.

That's it!
Push, glide, slide.
That's skating!

"Your turn, Claire."
I take a deep breath . . .
and *push* off.

Glide. A little *wibble*.

Slide. A little *wobble*.

Push *glide* slide.

"Look!" says Olivia, surprised. "She's skating!"

I am! I fly across the ice like a graceful swan.

"Go, Claire! Go, Claire!" chant the Snowplows.

Push *glide* slide.
Closer and closer . . .

BOOM!

Scribble scrabble up.

Push . . .
glide . . .
slide!

I touch the rail.
I did it!

"Hooray!" cheer the Snowplows.

"Good job, Claire," says Miss Nicole. "And good job, Snowplows. See you next week!"

We *wibble* *wobble* off the ice.

One of the hockey boys shoves past me.

"You know why you're a Snowplow?" he asks again.

And suddenly, I do!

"'Cause Snowplows work hard," I tell him.

"Yeah," Olivia butts in.
"Make way for the Snowplows!"
She gives me a smile and a high
five.

"See you next week." Olivia
waves.
"See you."

I change my skates for my shoes and *wibble wobble* off to find Mom.

Skating is hard. I feel like I skated to the North Pole and back!

Someday soon, though,
I'll have those white skates . . .
and then I'll—

jump,

and leap . . .

and twirl!